Sharks
up Close

Discovery
EDUCATION™

Discovery EDUCATION™

© 2011 Discovery Communications, LLC. **Discovery Education**™ and the **Discovery Education** logo are trademarks of Discovery Communications, LLC, used under license. All rights reserved.

Published by **Australian Geographic**
An imprint of Bauer Media Ltd.
54 Park Street, Sydney, NSW 2000
Telephone (02) 9263 9813,
Fax (02) 9263 9810
Email editorial@ausgeo.com.au
www.australiangeographic.com.au

Australian Geographic customer service
1300 555 176
(local call rate within Australia)
+61 2 8667 5295 from overseas
This edition published by
Australian Geographic in 2013

Conceived and produced by
Weldon Owen Pty Ltd
59–61 Victoria Street, McMahons Point
Sydney NSW 2060, Australia

Copyright © 2011 Weldon Owen Pty Ltd

WELDON OWEN PTY LTD
Managing Director Kay Scarlett
Creative Director Sue Burk
Publisher Helen Bateman
Senior Vice President,
International Sales Stuart Laurence
Sales Manager, North America
Ellen Towell
Administration Manager,
International Sales Kristine Ravn

Editor Madeleine Jennings
Copy Editors Barbara McClenahan,
Bronwyn Sweeney, Shan Wolody
Editorial Assistant Natalie Ryan
Design Managers Michelle Cutler,
Kathryn Morgan
Designer Karen Sagovac

Images Manager Trucie Henderson
Picture Research Tracey Gibson
Pre-press Operator Linda Benton
Production Director Todd Rechner
Production and Pre-press Controller
Mike Crowton

Consultant George McKay

ISBN: 978-174245173-2

Printed and bound in China by 1010 Printing Int Ltd.

A WELDON OWEN PRODUCTION

Sharks
up Close

David Stephens

Australian
GEOGRAPHIC

Contents

Fish with attitude

Sharks are a type of fish. Unlike other fish, sharks live for 40 years or more and are born ready to hunt for food. Sharks have a light skeleton that is made of soft cartilage instead of bone. Their skin is rough like sandpaper, not scaly and slippery like other fish.

Zebra shark

Caudal fin

First dorsal fin

Second dorsal fin

Chain catshark

Anal fin

Pelvic fin

Whale shark

This gentle giant is the world's largest living fish, and will often allow divers to swim alongside it.

Oceanic whitetip

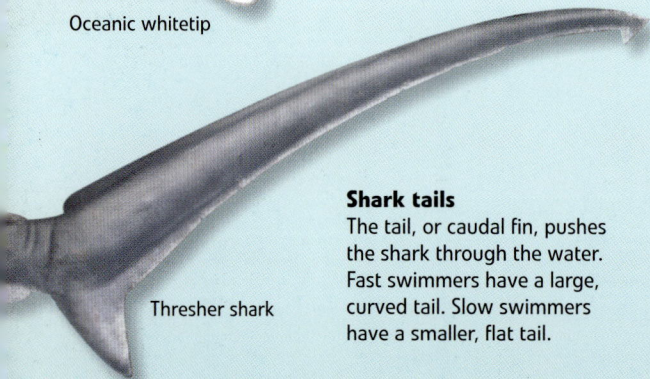

Shark tails

The tail, or caudal fin, pushes the shark through the water. Fast swimmers have a large, curved tail. Slow swimmers have a smaller, flat tail.

Thresher shark

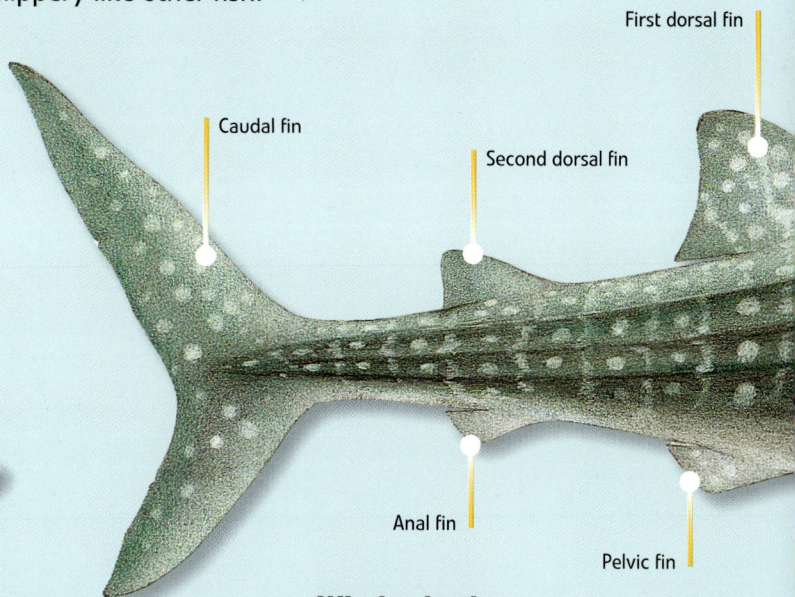

That's Amazing!

Fishermen have reported spotting huge whale sharks that are one and a half times the length of a regular school bus.

Horn shark

Blacktip reef shark

Great white shark

Shark fins

These are necessary for a shark's buoyancy and lift. They also help sharks to accelerate, brake and turn while swimming.

Sharks come in all sizes, ranging from the 18-centimetre spined pygmy shark to the 12-metre whale shark.

Gill slits

Eye

Frilled shark

Mouth

Spined pygmy shark

Pectoral fin

False catshark

Shark snouts

The shape of these tells us how a shark feeds: digging in the ocean floor, snapping at passing fish or cracking open shellfish.

Filter feeder

The whale shark sucks water in to its mouth, then filters it out through its gills, capturing tiny marine creatures to eat.

Black dogfish shark

Evolution

About 240 million years before dinosaurs were roaming the Earth, odd-looking shark ancestors hunted the oceans. Some of these sharks had curly teeth, while others had strange bristles on their head.

Evolution time line

How sharks evolved during ancient periods

* mya = million years ago

280 mya *Helicoprion*
This shark had a spiral set of teeth at the end of its lower jaw.

408 mya
In the Devonian period, fish diversified. The *Ctenacanthus* had spines in front of its dorsal fins.

505 mya
During the Ordovician period, sharks evolved from this thelodont.

550 mya
In the Cambrian period, animals with shells and jawless fish evolved. Trilobites looked like giant bugs.

435 mya
The first bony fish, such as this *Nostolepsis*, appeared during the Silurian period.

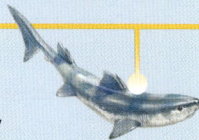

360 mya
The scissor-toothed shark evolved during the Carboniferous period.

370 mya *Cladoselache*
This species was unusual among ancient sharks because of its long keel fins.

320 mya *Stethacanthus*
The male had a 'scrub brush' on its head and first dorsal fin, which was possibly used during mating.

180 mya *Hybodus*
With sturdy spines in front of the dorsal fins, this shark looked like a cross between a tuna and a shark.

286 mya
In the Permian period, many creatures became extinct. Eel-like sharks survived in ancient rivers.

208 mya
In the Jurassic period, first rays evolved from flat sharks, such as this *Protospinax*.

65 mya
During the Cenozoic era, modern humans evolved. Megalodon dominated the ocean.

248 mya
Early dinosaurs appeared in the Triassic period. This *Nothosaurus* could hunt fish.

144 mya
During the Cretaceous period, *Tyrannosaurus* ruled the Earth and *Cretoxyrhina* ruled the oceans.

The giant Megalodon was 16 metres long. It could swallow five humans in one gulp and each razor-sharp tooth was the size of a man's hand.

FOSSILIZED SHARK TEETH

Hard teeth make excellent fossils. Since very few fossils of the cartilage skeleton are ever found, scientists guess the appearance of the rest of the shark from teeth fossils.

Types of sharks

There are more than 400 species of sharks in the oceans. Scientists have divided them into eight groups, or orders. These orders are based on classifications relating to shark features, such as the number of gills and the shape of teeth.

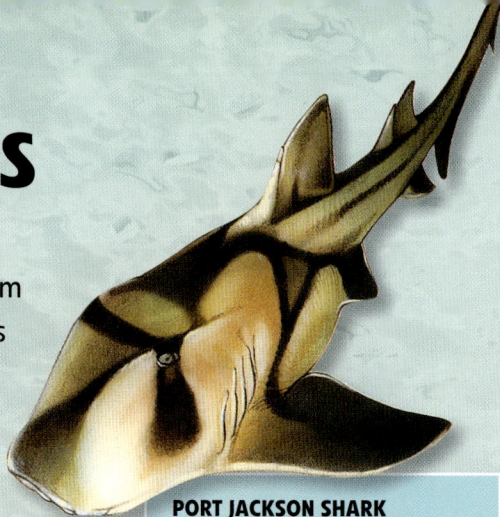

PORT JACKSON SHARK

ORDER: Heterodontiformes

SIZE: 1.7 metres

DIET: Sea urchins, starfish, barnacles and sea snails

HABITAT: Southern Australian oceans, from tidal to continental depths

ANGEL SHARK

ORDER: Squatiniformes

SIZE: 2 metres

DIET: Small fish, crustaceans, squid and molluscs

HABITAT: Bottom dwellers in warm oceans

BROADNOSE SHARK

ORDER: Hexanchiformes

SIZE: 3 metres

DIET: Larger animals such as sharks, rays, seals and seabirds

HABITAT: Temperate to tropical seas at continental shelf edges

BRAMBLE SHARK

ORDER: Squaliformes

SIZE: Up to 3 metres

DIET: A variety of bottom prey

HABITAT: Found at depths around 900 metres

HAMMERHEAD SHARK

ORDER: Carcharhiniformes

SIZE: 1.5 metres, but some are over 5 metres

DIET: Rays, other sharks, octopus and squid

HABITAT: Mostly warm coastal regions over the continental shelf and drop-off

ORNATE WOBBEGONG SHARK

ORDER: Orectolobiformes

SIZE: Up to 3.7 metres

DIET: Bottom fish, crabs, octopus and lobsters

HABITAT: Coral reefs and rocky or sandy seabeds

SHORTFIN MAKO SHARK

ORDER: Lamniformes

SIZE: About 2.5 metres, but can reach 3.7 metres

DIET: Schooling fish such as tuna, mackerel and swordfish

HABITAT: Migrates 2,500 kilometres seasonally from coastal waters to ocean depths

SAWSHARK

ORDER: Pristiophoriformes

SIZE: 1.5 metres

DIET: Small fish, crustaceans and squid

HABITAT: Continental shelves over gravel, mud or sandy bottoms

Inside the perfect predator

As well as a heart, brain, stomach and kidneys similar to humans, sharks also have gills for breathing underwater and a liver filled with oil that helps to keep them afloat. Extra blood vessels in its swimming muscles, brain and eyes keep sharks alert and ready for action.

Inside a salmon shark

Salmon sharks live in the cold North Pacific Ocean, where they eat their favourite food, salmon. They have extra networks of blood vessels to keep their blood warm.

Reproductive organs

Intestines

CARTILAGE SKELETON

A shark's skeleton is made of soft cartilage similar to human ears. Cartilage is lighter than bone, and makes it easier for a shark to swim.

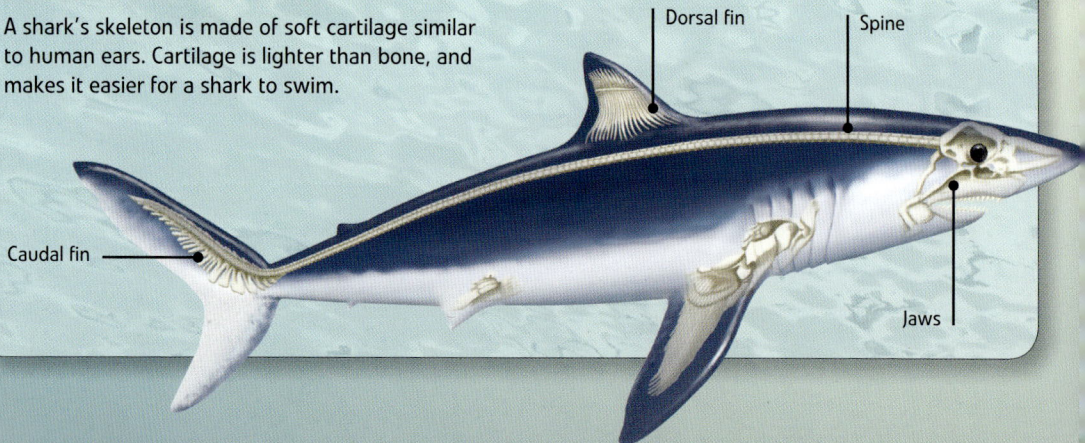

Dorsal fin

Spine

Caudal fin

Jaws

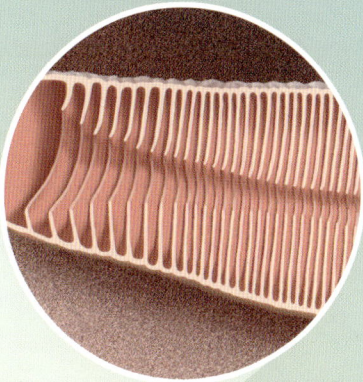

Spiral valve
Sharks have short intestines, so the inside is made like a spiral to provide a large surface area for digesting food.

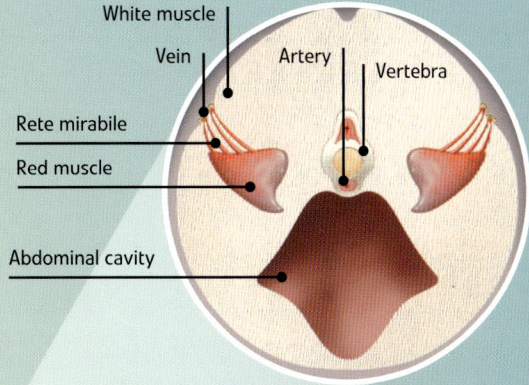

White muscle
Vein
Artery
Vertebra
Rete mirabile
Red muscle
Abdominal cavity

Expanding stomach

Heart

Gill slits

Brain

Rete mirabile
This cross-section shows two of the four networks of fine blood vessels that warm cold blood coming from the gills. A salmon shark can keep its blood temperature at a comfortable 26°C, despite ice-cold waters.

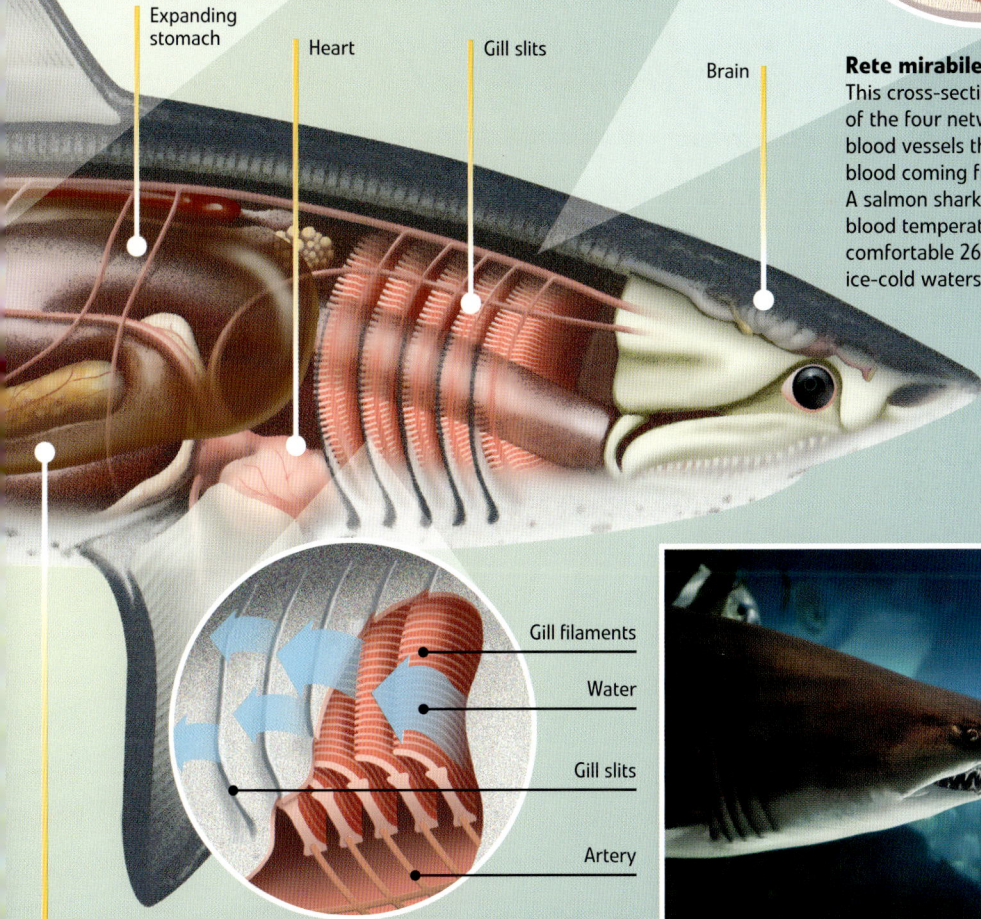

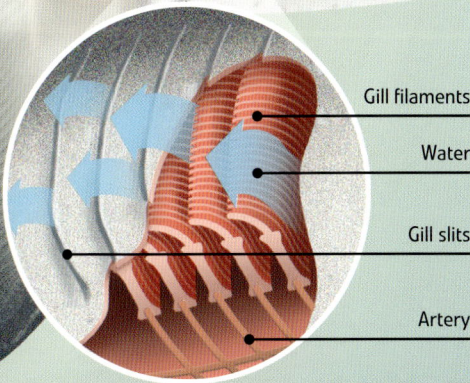

Gill filaments

Water

Gill slits

Artery

Liver

How gills work
Water enters the shark's mouth and flows out across the gill filaments. Blood in the gills flows in the opposite direction, picking up oxygen from the water.

Gills up close
Sharks have five to seven gill slits, and sometimes an extra one called a spiracle. The spiracle allows a shark to breathe with a mouth filled with food. Most sharks need to keep moving to breathe.

Nowhere to hide

S harks have an awesome array of senses. They hear and feel a thrashing fish 500 metres away, and their directional sense of smell detects blood in the water up to 25 metres away. Their excellent eyesight allows them to see in low light and, up close, electrical sensors in their snout guide their final, fatal bite.

HAMMERHEAD VISION

Hammerhead sharks have eyes on either side of their wing-shaped head. This gives great side vision, but they must swing their head from side to side to see forward.

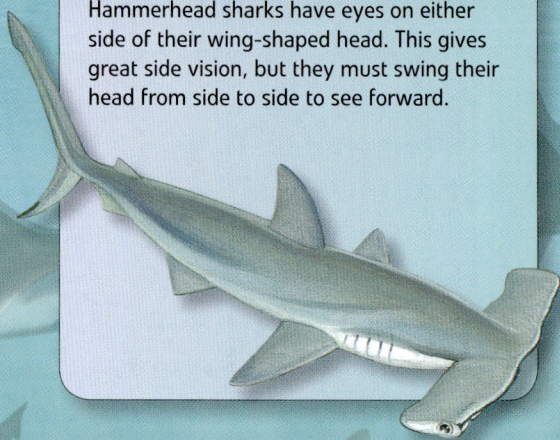

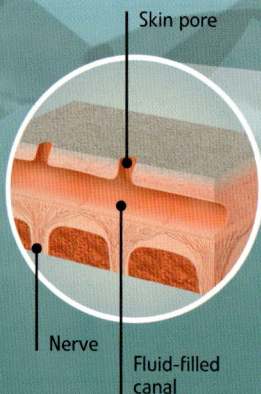

A shark's sensory trail

Here is how a shark uses its senses to hunt a bluefin tuna.

Skin pore

1 Hearing

Tiny holes on the head connect to the inner ear, which detects sound waves in the water. Semicircular canals in the ear maintain balance.

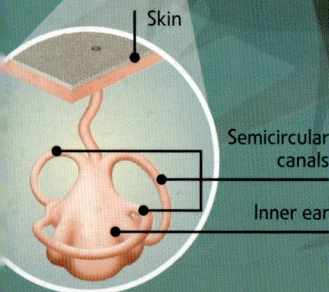

Nerve

Fluid-filled canal

2 Smell

Inside the shark's nostrils, water containing the tuna scent flows across a group of sensing membranes called lamellae.

Skin

Semicircular canals

Inner ear

5 Electroreceptors

The ampullae of Lorenzini are jelly-filled pits on the shark's snout. They contain sensors that detect minute electrical currents caused when muscles contract. This shark can sense the tuna's heart beating.

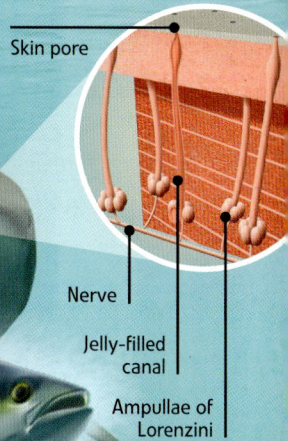

Skin pore

Nerve

Jelly-filled canal

Ampullae of Lorenzini

4 Pressure detection

Under the skin is the lateral line – a system of fluid-filled canals that act like motion sensors. They detect the smallest pressure changes in the water.

6 Taste

Shark taste buds are in its mouth and gullet, not on the tongue like human taste buds.

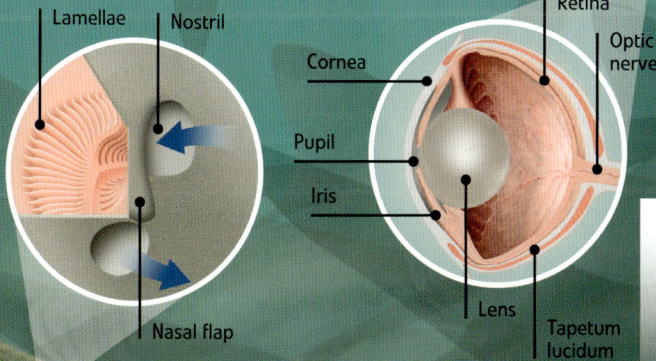

Lamellae   Nostril

Cornea

Pupil

Iris

Retina

Optic nerve

Nasal flap

Lens

Tapetum lucidum

3 Vision

Shark eyes have a special lining called tapetum lucidum to improve vision at dawn and dusk, when the shark hunts.

When hunting, the fastest swimming shark is the shortfin mako. It reaches speeds of 50 kilometres per hour.

Bite time

No escape
A shark's cartilage jaws are hinged just behind the head and held in place with powerful muscles.

When a shark attacks, it moves its jaw forward to allow teeth to do maximum damage to its prey. A tiger shark can bite down with a force of 422 kilograms per square centimetre. If a shark breaks or loses teeth, another row pops into place.

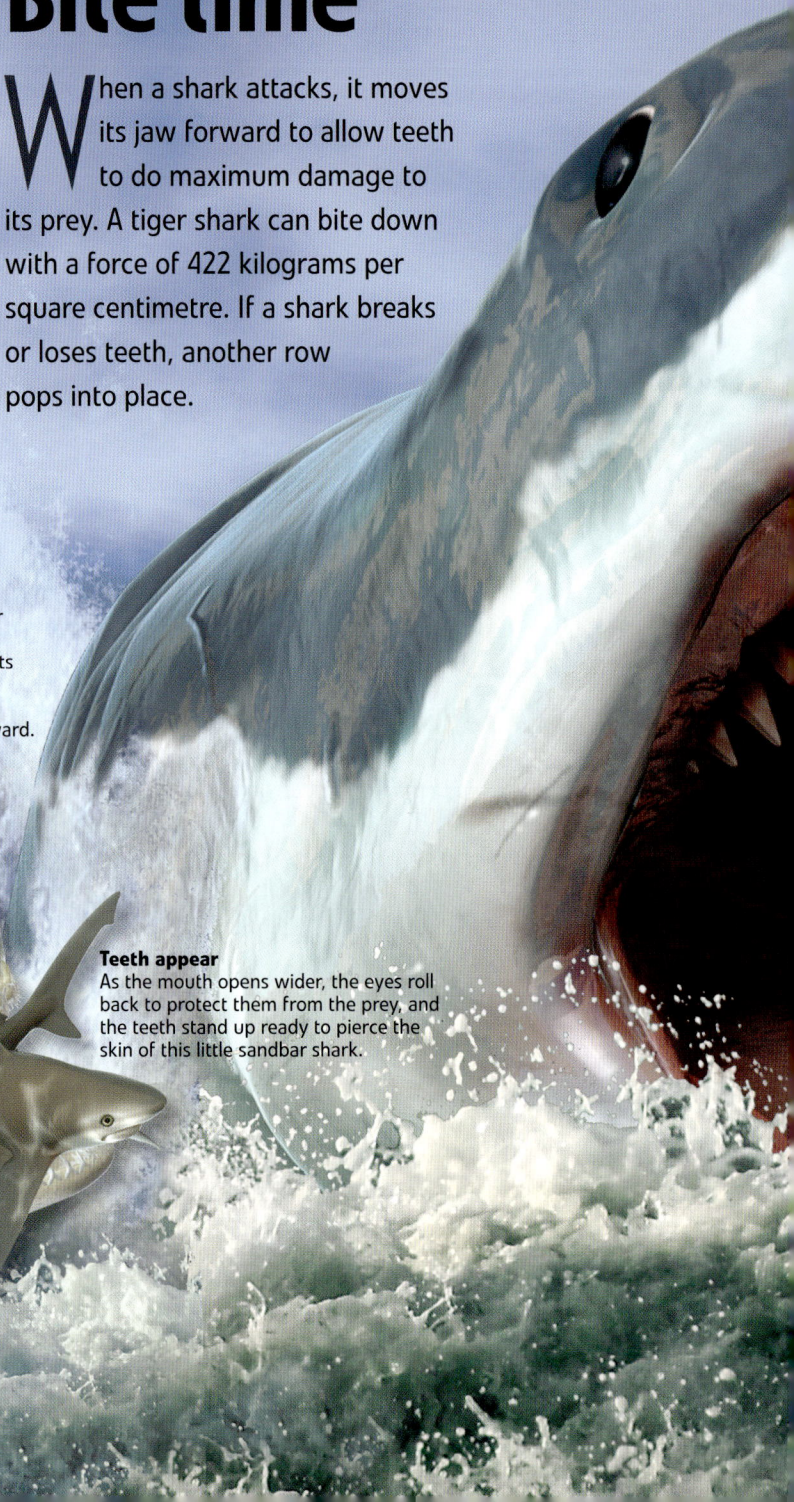

Jaw relaxes
As it prepares to bite, a shark's jaw relaxes and its mouth starts to open.

Jaw moves forward
As the lower jaw drops, the snout tilts up and the upper jaw pushes forward.

Teeth appear
As the mouth opens wider, the eyes roll back to protect them from the prey, and the teeth stand up ready to pierce the skin of this little sandbar shark.

Great teeth for a great white shark

This shark is the owner of the world's largest shark teeth. When it grabs its prey, it shakes its head from side to side so the razor-sharp teeth act like mini saws.

A TOOTH FOR EVERY MEAL

Sharks' teeth are tailored to suit the prey on which they feed.

Tiger shark
Sawing and smashing teeth of the tiger shark can tackle a turtle shell.

Pale goblin shark
Spearing teeth of the pale goblin shark can pin down wriggling squid.

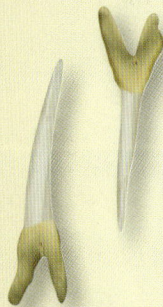

Kitefin shark
Serrated lower and hooked upper teeth of the kitefin shark are ideal for grabbing whole fish.

Great white shark
Sawlike teeth of the great white shark slice up seals and other large prey.

Filter feeders

Only three species of shark are filter feeders – the basking, the whale and the megamouth. The megamouth has light-producing organs around its mouth to attract plankton, while the basking shark swims with its mouth open.

Basking shark

Megamouth shark

Shark diet

Sharks usually eat meat, although some sharks will eat just about anything. Scientists who examined the contents of tiger shark stomachs after they were caught found everything from shoes to buckets and, one time, even a suit of armour.

Blue shark banquet

When millions of market squid swarm together to find mates, blue sharks will swim through the middle and gulp down huge mouthfuls.

Open wide

Whale sharks are filter feeders. They suck in huge amounts of water containing small marine creatures, push the water out through their gills and swallow the sieved food.

WHAT'S ON THE MENU?

Because sharks are at the top of the ocean food chain, they are equipped to eat anything.

Lobster
A hard shell will not protect a lobster from hungry sharks.

Turtle
A turtle's shell is no match for a tiger shark.

Seal
Great white sharks prefer to eat seals.

Ray
The ray is a favourite of the hammerhead shark.

Seabird
Resting seabirds make a change from seafood.

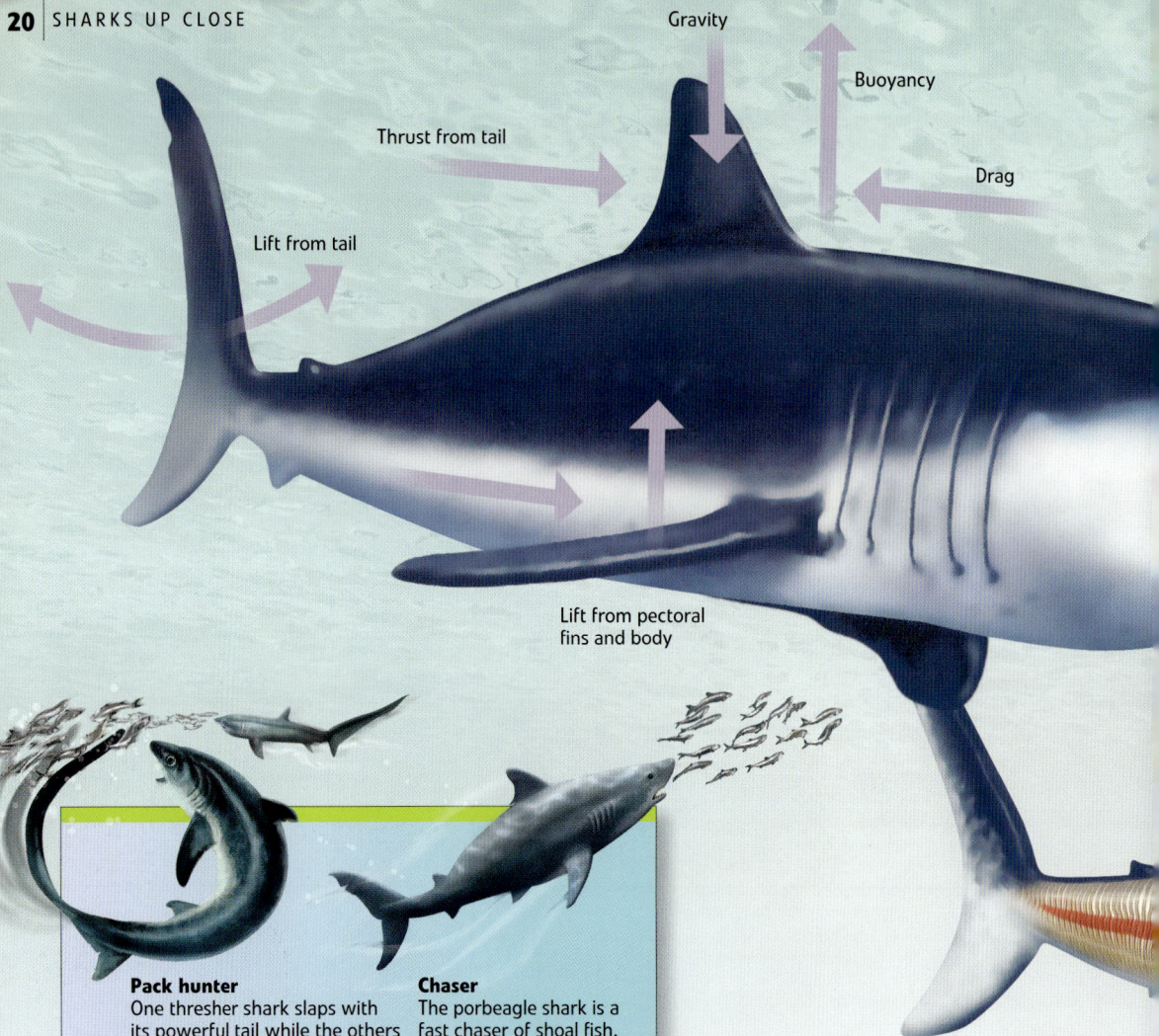

Gravity

Buoyancy

Thrust from tail

Drag

Lift from tail

Lift from pectoral
fins and body

Pack hunter
One thresher shark slaps with
its powerful tail while the others
pick off the stunned fish.

Chaser
The porbeagle shark is a
fast chaser of shoal fish.

MASTERS
OF THE HUNT

Whether they are a chaser,
digger, pack hunter or
ambush predator, a shark's
body is adapted to its
hunting style.

Camouflage
Half buried in sand,
a camouflaged angel
shark lies waiting to
pounce on its prey.

Digger
A longnose sawshark
digs in the sand to
root out fish.

How a shark swims
Sharks use a waving motion
to push through the water.

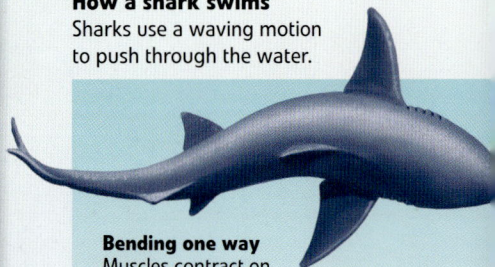

Bending one way
Muscles contract on
one side of the spine,
bending the body.

Built for speed

Shaped like a torpedo
The shortfin mako has the body and crescent tail of a high-speed underwater athlete.

Most sharks must keep swimming to force water over their gills. If they stop, they will suffocate. Buoyancy and lift provided by its liver, pectoral fin and tail help the shark resist the pull of gravity and prevent it from sinking. Thrust from the tail drives the shark forward against the drag of the water. Even the tough, scaly skin is designed to reduce friction.

Mako sharks have the muscle power to leap from the water like a missile. They have frightened many fishermen by actually landing in their boat.

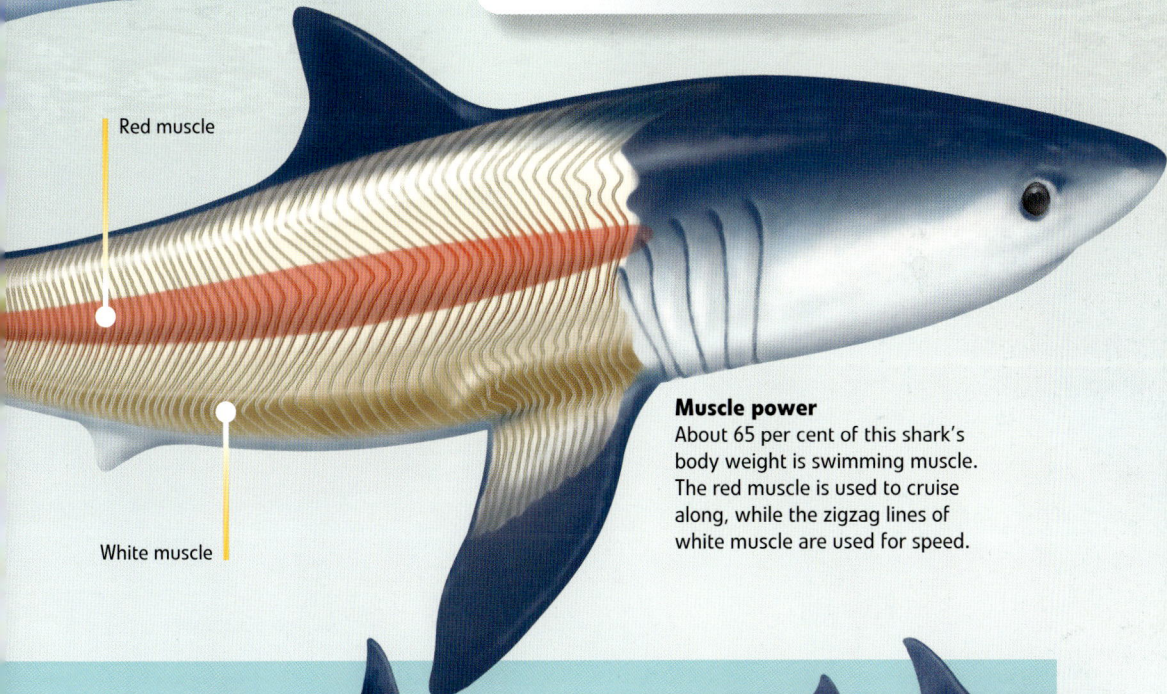

Red muscle

White muscle

Muscle power
About 65 per cent of this shark's body weight is swimming muscle. The red muscle is used to cruise along, while the zigzag lines of white muscle are used for speed.

Thrusting forward
The body straightens and the tail thrusts the shark forward.

Bending the other way
Muscles on the other side of the spine contract and the body bends the other way.

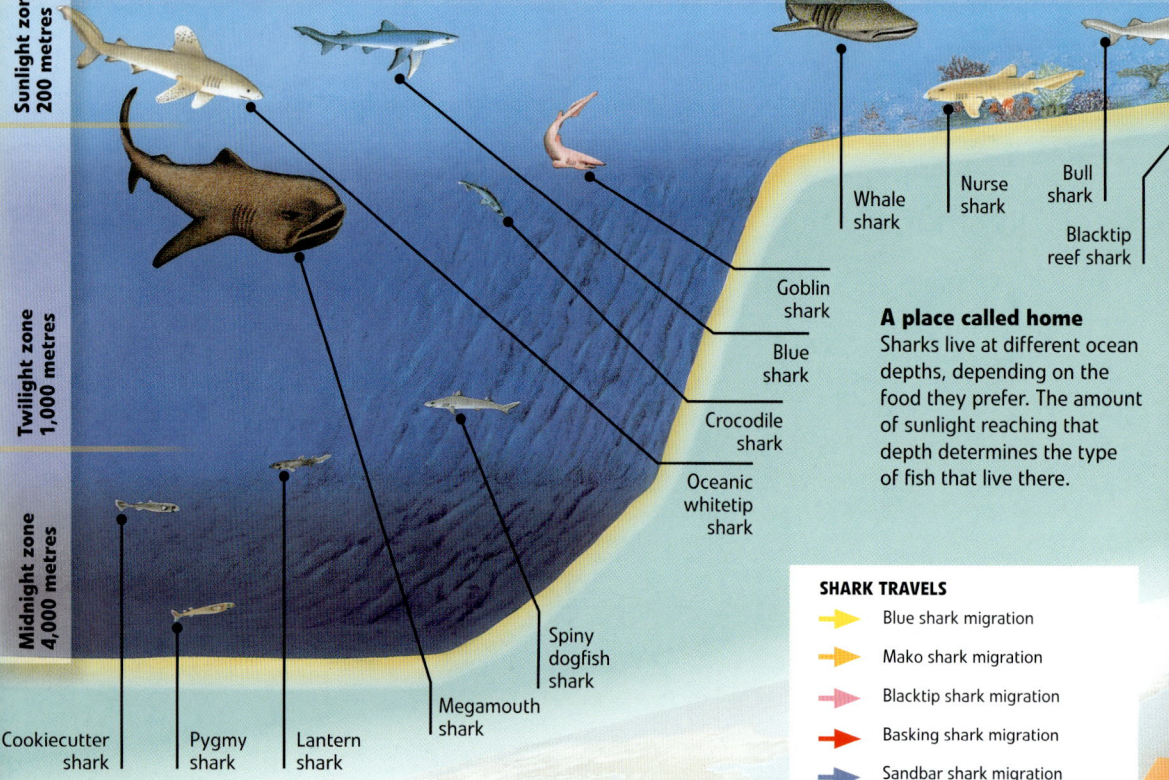

Whale shark

Nurse shark

Bull shark

Blacktip reef shark

Goblin shark

Blue shark

Crocodile shark

Oceanic whitetip shark

A place called home
Sharks live at different ocean depths, depending on the food they prefer. The amount of sunlight reaching that depth determines the type of fish that live there.

Spiny dogfish shark

Megamouth shark

Cookiecutter shark

Pygmy shark

Lantern shark

SHARK TRAVELS

Blue shark migration

Mako shark migration

Blacktip shark migration

Basking shark migration

Sandbar shark migration

Nurse shark distribution (no migration)

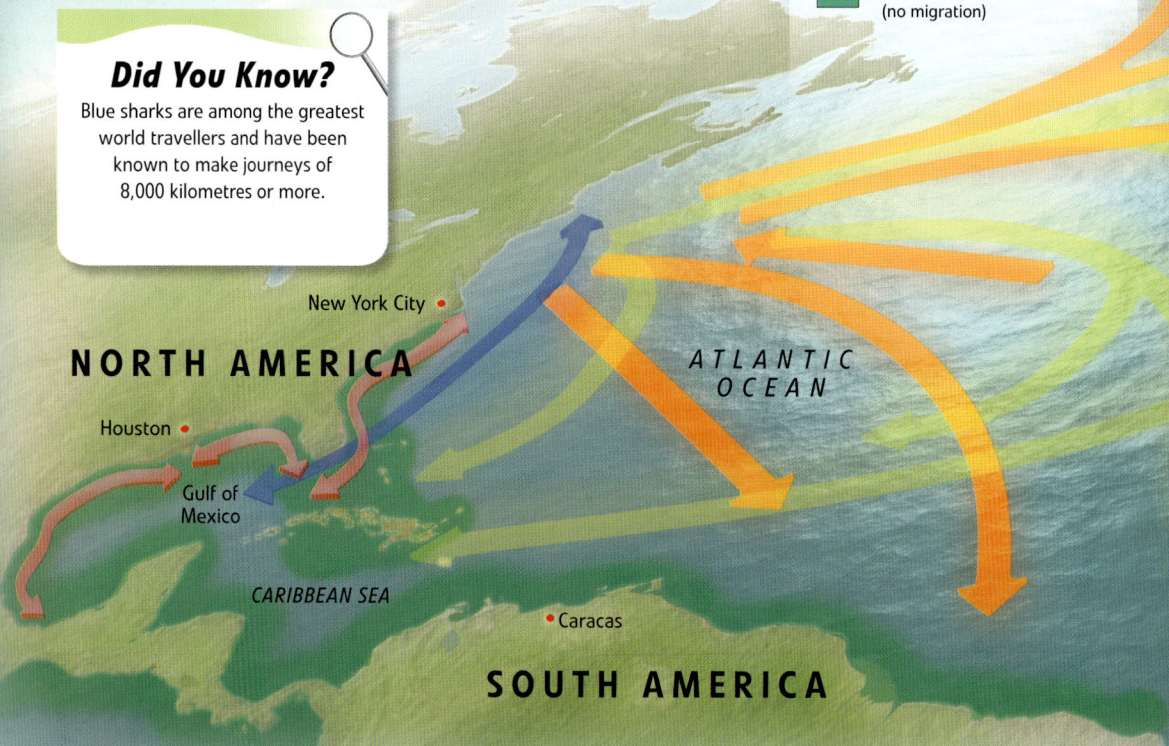

Did You Know?
Blue sharks are among the greatest world travellers and have been known to make journeys of 8,000 kilometres or more.

New York City

NORTH AMERICA

Houston

Gulf of Mexico

ATLANTIC OCEAN

CARIBBEAN SEA

Caracas

SOUTH AMERICA

Habitats

Sharks can be found in almost any marine environment. Some prefer swimming in deep waters, while others enjoy shallow, coastal areas. Some travel thousands of kilometres to find a mate or to follow migrating fish. Others look for water that is just the right temperature.

HOME FOR SHARK PUPS

Mangrove forests that grow on the edge of oceans are the birthplace of many water creatures, including sharks. Conservationists are trying to stop these important breeding grounds disappearing as a result of coastal development.

London
Paris

EUROPE

Madrid

Rabat

AFRICA

MEDITERRANEAN SEA

ASIA

Migration mysteries

Until recently, scientists had no idea how far sharks travelled. Today, sharks are tagged with tiny satellite positioning devices, and studies show that they make journeys of thousands of kilometres around the globe.

ATLANTIC OCEAN

Dakar

Up close and personal

Much of what is known about sharks has come from studying dead ones. Scientists today, however, are more interested in observing live ones. This requires a great deal of patience because it is impossible to swim with sharks 24 hours a day. Sharks are tagged and tracked. This is a risky business but there are many ways to protect the observer.

Photographing sharks
Waving your arms at a shark is like an invitation to lunch. Undersea photographers keep their bodies very still so the sharks do not feel threatened.

Did You Know?
Many sharks go into a trancelike state and become immobile when flipped onto their back. Once righted, they swim off as if nothing happened.

KEEPING SHARKS AT BAY

There are a few safety devices to chase off nosey sharks should you happen to be in the water with one.

US Navy shark bag
This bag is designed for surviving at sea.

Shark-proof vest
Specially designed life vests have a chemical repellent.

Protective Oceanic Device
Attached to flippers or a surfboard, protective oceanic devices (PODs) produce a strong electric field that repels sharks.

Tagging sharks

A netted shark is pulled close to the boat and a tracking tag is attached. Sometimes tags are attached by a scuba diver using a long pole or special harpoon gun.

Into the depths

Scientists use a submersible to study sharks in water depths down to 5 kilometres. At these dark depths, sharks such as the spined pygmy shark have light-producing cells on their underside.

?... You decide

More than 100 million sharks die in fishing nets every year, and their breeding grounds are being destroyed by human activity and pollution. Many sharks need to reach an age of between 10 and 20 years before they can breed, so it is no wonder they are under threat. On the other hand, are they a threat to humans?

Trapped by nets
Sharks, rays and even dolphins often become tangled in fishing nets. Unable to swim, a shark will drown through lack of oxygen.

WHAT ARE THE ODDS?

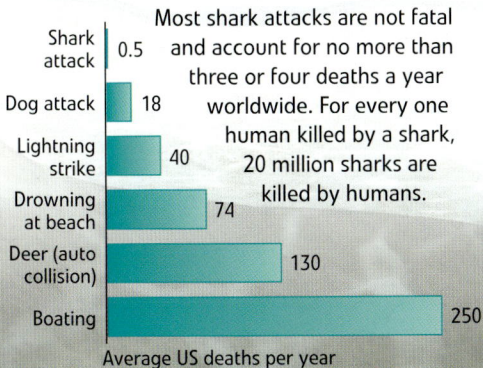

Most shark attacks are not fatal and account for no more than three or four deaths a year worldwide. For every one human killed by a shark, 20 million sharks are killed by humans.

	Average US deaths per year
Shark attack	0.5
Dog attack	18
Lightning strike	40
Drowning at beach	74
Deer (auto collision)	130
Boating	250

More curious than aggressive
Most sharks use their mouth to 'feel' things they do not understand. Experts believe that only the bull, great white, mako and tiger sharks are threatening to humans.

PRODUCTS TO DIE FOR

Sharks have been killed for use in medicine, food, cosmetics and other products.

Cosmetics
Shark oil is used in some lipsticks, creams and lotions.

Food
Shark meat is eaten, but often only the dorsal fin is cut off to make an expensive Asian soup.

Medicine
The clear covering that protects a shark's eye is used to repair damaged human eyes.

Dietary supplements
Sharks' liver oil contains vitamin A and is used in vitamin pills.

Endangered

More than 60 species of shark are under threat of possible extinction. Overfishing and being caught in nets and long drag lines are causing a steep drop in shark numbers. Sharks are the oceans' top predators. Without them, the balance of life in the oceans will be seriously affected.

BASKING SHARK

This harmless shark has a slow reproduction rate and has been overfished for its huge liver.

STRIPED SMOOTH-HOUND SHARK

This small shark is easily caught in fishing nets and has almost disappeared from its home waters off South America.

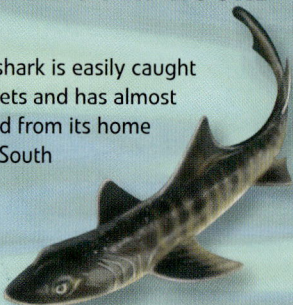

GREY NURSE SHARK

This shark has only two pups every two years, so even killing just a few adults affects their numbers.

ANGEL SHARK

Trawler nets that scrape along the ocean floor capture many angel sharks. They are mostly thrown back but usually do not survive.

DAGGERNOSE SHARK

This shark has been overfished in its home waters, off the coast of Venezuela, and has now almost disappeared.

GULPER SHARK

This shark prefers deep waters. It gives birth only every two years. It is fished heavily around its native area, Taiwan.

GREAT WHITE SHARK

This shark has only one pup every two to three years and does not breed until it is 10 years old. In the past 50 years, the drop in population numbers is estimated at between 60 and 95 per cent, making the species very vulnerable.

Mix and match

In this book you will find many interesting facts about different sharks. On this page they have all been mixed up. You have to match the shark on the left with an interesting fact about them on the right. The answers are at the bottom of the page.

A

Whale shark

Megalodon

Pygmy shark

Shortfin mako shark

Great white shark

Porbeagle shark

Blue shark

Daggernose shark

Hammerhead shark

B

wing-shaped head

fast chaser of shoal fish

migrates the greatest distance

largest teeth

lives near Venezuela

filter feeder

fastest shark

largest extinct shark

smallest shark

Answers: whale shark – filter feeder; Megalodon – largest extinct shark; pygmy shark – smallest shark; shortfin mako shark – fastest shark; great white shark – largest teeth; porbeagle shark – fast chaser of shoal fish; blue shark – migrates the greatest distance; daggernose shark – lives near Venezuela; hammerhead shark – has a wing-shaped head

Glossary

abdominal cavity
the body part that holds the stomach, liver and intestines

ampullae of Lorenzini
jelly-filled sacs connected to the snout of a shark that can detect very weak electrical fields, as weak as half a billionth of a volt

anal fin
a stabilizing fin near the anus of a fish

buoyancy
an upward-acting force caused by water pressure that helps things stay afloat

cartilage
a type of body tissue that is not as hard and rigid as bone, but is more rigid and less flexible than muscle

caudal fin
the tail fin of any fish that is used for pushing it through the water

dorsal fin
fin located on the back of a fish

fossil
the preserved remains of any living creature that has been dug up

gills
a body part found in all fish that extracts dissolved oxygen from water and releases carbon dioxide. It is used by a shark for breathing.

lamellae
fine layers of membranes that improve a shark's ability to smell

lateral line
a fluid-filled canal lined with tiny hairlike receptors used as a sensing organ to detect vibrations and movement in the water. The lateral line is located just under the skin of sharks.

migration
the regular movement around the world of animal groups, often in search of food or desirable breeding grounds

pectoral fins
located on either side of a fish's body, the pectoral fins are like a fish's arms. Some fish use them for walking on, others use them for flying, such as the flying fish.

pelvic fins
located on the underside of a fish, near its belly, these are the equivalent to hind legs on a four-legged animal

plankton
tiny drifting animal and plant organisms that are a source of food for fish and some sharks

POD
an acronym for Protective Oceanic Device. This device emits a small electric current that is said to repel sharks.

rete mirabile
a network of fine blood vessels found in many different animals. It is used by fish to regulate their body temperature.

submersible
a commercial or non-military device for travelling underwater, sometimes to great depths. They can be manned or unmanned.

tapetum lucidum
a layer of tissue in the eyes of a shark that improves the shark's ability to see in low light

Index

Credits and acknowledgements
KEY tl=top left; bl=bottom left; br=bottom right

CBT = Corbis; iS = istockphoto.com; SH = Shutterstock; TPL = photolibrary.com

7bl SH; **9**br TPL; **13**br SH; **24**tl iS; **25**tl CBT

All illustrations copyright Weldon Owen Pty Ltd